Samuel French Acting Edition

The Evolution of Mann

Music and Lyrics by
Douglas J. Cohen

Book and Lyrics by
Dan Elish

I0591815

Based on the novel Nine Wives *by*
Dan Elish

SAMUELFRENCH.COM   SAMUELFRENCH.CO.UK

FOR PRODUCTION ENQUIRIES

UNITED STATES AND CANADA
Info@SamuelFrench.com
1-866-598-8449

UNITED KINGDOM AND EUROPE
Plays@SamuelFrench.co.uk
020-7255-4302

Each title is subject to availability from Samuel French, depending upon country of performance. Please be aware that THE EVOLUTION OF MANN may not be licensed by Samuel French in your territory. Professional and amateur producers should contact the nearest Samuel French office or licensing partner to verify availability.

MUSIC USE NOTE

Licensees are solely responsible for obtaining formal written permission from copyright owners to use copyrighted music in the performance of this play and are strongly cautioned to do so. If no such permission is obtained by the licensee, then the licensee must use only original music that the licensee owns and controls. Licensees are solely responsible and liable for all music clearances and shall indemnify the copyright owners of the play(s) and their licensing agent, Samuel French, against any costs, expenses, losses and liabilities arising from the use of music by licensees. Please contact the appropriate music licensing authority in your territory for the rights to any incidental music.

IMPORTANT BILLING AND CREDIT REQUIREMENTS

If you have obtained performance rights to this title, please refer to your licensing agreement for important billing and credit requirements.

NINE WIVES was first performed in February 2012 in a workshop produced by Larry Hirschhorn and directed by Chip Klose. The cast included Zachary Prince, Sarah Stiles, Heidi Blickenstaff, Patti Murin, and Andrew Kober.

NINE WIVES was chosen to be part of the Goodspeed Festival of New Musicals in 2013. Originally developed by Larry Hirschhorn and Jayson Raitt.

MANN AND WIFE was originally produced at Lyric Theatre of Oklahoma (Michael Baron, Producing Artistic Director; Paula Stover, Managing Director) on February 3, 2016. The performance was directed by Michael Baron, with set design by Adam Koch, costume design by Jeffrey Meek, lighting design by Art Whaley, and sound design by Maurizio M. D'Errico. The stage manager was Rickelle Williams. The cast was as follows:

HENRY MANN. . . . . Zachary Prince
CHRISTINE / TAMAR / SHEILA / OTHERS. . . . . Liz Shivener
GLENN / OTHERS . . . . Mateja Govitch

THE EVOLUTION OF MANN opened Off Broadway at Nancy Manocherian's The Cell (Kira Simring, Artistic Director), in association with La Vie Productions, EOM Developmental LLC, Conway Partners LP, Anthony E. Hull, and Truscott Associates LLC, and associate producers Liz Flemming and Maggie Snyder, on October 4, 2018 in New York City. The performance was directed by Joe Barros, with associate direction by Brian Reager, set design by Libby Stadstad, costume design by Siena Zöe Allen, lighting design by Chris Steckel, orchestrations by Matt Aument, projection design by Nathan Scheuer, and casting by WOJCIK/SEAY. The music supervisor was Vadim Feichtner, and the music director was Eric Svejcar. The production stage manager was Kayla Santos. The cast was as follows:

HENRY MANN. . . . . Max Crumm
GWEN. . . . . Leslie Hiatt
SHEILA / TAMAR / CHRISTINE / MRS. MANN / OTHERS . . . . . . Allie Trimm
UNDERSTUDIES . . . . Jesse Manocherian, Liz Flemming

CHARACTERS

Actor One

HENRY MANN – Our eager and romantically-challenged hero, thirty-two years old, recently invited to his ex-fiancée's wedding; legal proofreader by night, frustrated writer by day. Henry is someone with one foot rooted in the past who spends much of his time projecting into the future.

Actor Two

GWEN – Henry's best friend and roommate; gay, recently split from her wife.

HARVEY TRITONE – A lounge singer.

JIM – An ex-boyfriend.

JAY GATSBY

TIMES SQUARE'S NAKED COWBOY

MRS. MANN – Henry's mother.

Actor Three

SHEILA – Henry's ex-fiancée; beautiful, refined, but in love with someone else.

TAMAR – Henry's current love interest; charming, vivacious, but with a somewhat checkered romantic past.

CHRISTINE – A sweet third grade teacher with a great jump shot and a barely perceptible unibrow.

DAISY BUCHANAN – The fictional heroine of *The Great Gatsby*.

NATALIE – A girl in the park.

MELLOW VOICE – The MC at the Sleepy Wheel, a folk bar.

WOMAN'S VOICE – A mystery woman who leaves forthright phone messages.

SETTING

Various locations in and around New York City

TIME

The Present

AUTHORS' NOTE

The authors are open to productions in which multiple actresses play all of these parts to accommodate a larger cast.

The show is written so that the actors have time to quickly change costumes between each appearance.

MUSICAL NUMBERS

"The Year Of The Weddings"	Henry, Gwen, Sheila
"She's My Wife"	Henry & Tamar
"The Tale Of The Otter"	Henry & Christine
"Hard"	Henry & Christine
"Settling Down"	Henry, Sheila, Gwen
"It's Only A First Date"	Christine
"What's The Matter With Henry?"	Gwen, Mrs. Mann, Henry, Tamar, Christine
"The Right Time To Propose"	Henry & Tamar
"Low Expectations"	Henry & Tamar
"The Green Light"	Jay Gatsby, Daisy Buchanan, Henry
"It's Only A First Date – Reprise"	Christine
"The Unromantic Things"	Gwen & Henry
"Keeping My Eye On The Ball"	Henry

Dedicated to our wives, Cathy and Andrea

Scene One

[MUSIC NO. 00 "OVERTURE"]

(A New York bachelor pad. As the lights rise and the music swells, **SHEILA***, a beautiful woman in a wedding dress, overlooks the proceedings, tosses out a wedding invitation, and watches it flutter to the floor. As* **SHEILA** *disappears, our hero,* **HENRY MANN***, wakes up on the couch, still in last night's suit. He is a nice-looking, thirty-two-year-old guy, well-meaning but still looking for answers. Despite all his foibles and bad calls, he has a good heart.)*

HENRY. *(Screams out from a dream.)* Sheila!

(A beat, sees the audience.)

Hi. I'm Henry Mann and you're not exactly catching me on my best day. You see, I just got through this thing I call "The Year of the Weddings." If you can believe it, that's twelve weddings in twelve months...and one of them was my *dad's*...to a thirty-year-old...that I used to date.

(A beat.)

What makes the whole thing painfully ironic is that this time last year I was still with Sheila, the love of my life...until she dumped me...about twenty seconds after I proposed. Which meant that I went to those aforementioned twelve weddings *alone*.

(A beat.)

It's difficult devoting so many weekends to other people's happiness. And besides, I just don't understand it. I'm thirty-two, a perfectly acceptable athlete, passably good-looking and disease-free. With everyone I know getting married, why can't I find a wife?

(Enter **GWEN**, *Henry's best friend and roommate.)*

GWEN. Why can't you find a wife?

[MUSIC NO. 01A "THE YEAR OF THE WEDDINGS (PT. 1)"]

HENRY. *(To audience.)* My best friend, Gwen.

GWEN. Need I remind you of your behavior last night?

HENRY. What? At the wedding?

GWEN.

> I THOUGHT I WAS THE CHILD IN THIS APARTMENT
> DIFFICULT, SELFISH, INSECURE
> BUT LAST NIGHT YOU ACHIEVED THE IMPOSSIBLE:
> YOU MADE *ME* LOOK MATURE

HENRY. I guess I've been acting out a bit, huh?

GWEN. A bit? You ate salmon with your bare hands. You proposed to Rabbi Linda!

HENRY. The rabbi?

GWEN. You asked the flower girl if she wanted to get stoned.

HENRY. Oh, god...

GWEN.

> YOU WERE DEEPLY DISGUSTING, YOU BROKE EV'RY RULE
> PERPETUALLY LUSTING, SO MIDDLE SCHOOL

HENRY.

> I WENT AFTER A GIRL WHO BELONGS IN A SHUL
> I really hit on the rabbi?

GWEN.

> YOU TOOK HER HAND AND DID THE HORA
> THEN UNSCROLLED HER TORAH

HENRY. Ouch!

GWEN.

> BOBBING AND WEAVING
> THE ROOM WAS YOUR PREY

HENRY.

MAYBE IT WAS A SORDID DISPLAY

HENRY & GWEN.

TACKLING THE BRIDESMAID WHO CAUGHT THE
BOUQUET

GWEN.

WE ALL AGREED YOU HIT YOUR STRIDE

DOING SHOTS WITH THE MOTHER OF THE BRIDE

HENRY.

OH GOD, BUT THIS WAS THE YEAR OF THE WEDDINGS

GWEN. I know.

HENRY.

TWELVE MONTHS TO FORGET

ANOTHER TUX TO TRY

ANOTHER TOASTER TO BUY

ANOTHER EVENING OF REGRET

GWEN. You bet.

HENRY & GWEN.

ALL THOSE IMPOSSIBLE WEDDINGS

WERE ANYTHING BUT FUN

HENRY.

THOSE DAYS ARE GONE

I'M MOVING ON

THANK GOD THEY'RE DONE

GWEN. Well...

HENRY. All right, Gwen. I've had my year of acting like a
jerk, but I'm officially ready to crawl out of the abyss.
And guess what? Good news! I have no more single
friends! Which means no more weddings!

GWEN. *(Seeing Sheila's invitation.)* Uh, not so fast, man.

HENRY.

SLAMMED IN THE FACE,

KICKED HARD IN THE SHINS,

BUT NOW IS THE TIME LIFE TRULY BEGINS

THIS TIME AROUND, THE GOOFY GUY WINS

GWEN. *(Holding out the invitation.)*

HOLD THAT THOUGHT

    DON'T EXHALE
    'TIL YOU SEE WHAT CAME IN THE MAIL

HENRY.

    GOODBYE TO THE YEAR OF THE WEDDINGS
    I GAVE ALL I COULD GIVE
    GONNA CLEAN UP MY ACT
    GONNA MAKE ME A PACT
    TO GET OFF MY BUTT AND LIVE

GWEN. Henry!

HENRY.

    I GOT THROUGH THE YEAR OF THE WEDDINGS
    PRAYED THAT IT WOULD PASS
    LIFE'S BEEN BLEAK
    A LOSING STREAK SINCE...

GWEN.

    OH GOD, DON'T GO THERE

HENRY.

    SINCE SHEILA...

GWEN.

    HENRY, STOP!

HENRY.

    SINCE SHEILA DUMPED MY SORRY ASS!

GWEN. Sheila. Funny you brought her up. Here you go.

    (She hands **HENRY** *an unopened invitation.)*

HENRY. What?

    SHE'S GETTING MARRIED?!

    (He rips open the invitation.)

  In three months? She invited me?!

GWEN. It would appear so.

HENRY. *(Reading.)* "To witness the union of two souls, Sheila Madison Kinney to Thor Arnold Rosenbaum."

    (To **GWEN.***)* The *Google* guy?

GWEN.

    YEP

HENRY. But she was supposed to marry me!

[MUSIC NO. 01B "THE YEAR OF THE WEDDINGS (PT. 2)"]

(The lights tighten on **HENRY** *as he goes into a dream.* **SHEILA** *enters. She's beautiful.)*

SHEILA. Hi, Henry.

GWEN. Henry! Stop it!

HENRY. *(To* **GWEN.***)* Shut up! It's my fantasy!

(Sings to **SHEILA.***)*

SHEILA!
MY BEST FRIEND AND MY BEST LOVER
SHELIA, SHEILA!
YOU WERE THE PERFECT BLEND
SHEILA!
THE DECAF TO MY CREAM, OH
WASP GODDESS OF MY DREAM
IN YOUR SANDALS FROM LANDS' END

SHEILA. Oh, Henry! I still love you. Sort of.

HENRY. How could you do it? How could you dump me for a guy named Thor?

SHEILA. Well, he's rich and handsome and funny and an absolute animal in the...

HENRY.

SHEILA!
FIVE LONG YEARS TOGETHER
AND NOW IT'S STORMY WEATHER
I HOPE YOU AND YOUR MILLIONAIRE GEEKBOY ROT IN
    HELL!

*(***SHEILA** *exits.)*

GWEN. So I take it you're not going?

HENRY. Of course I'm going. Look what it says here. Henry Mann and *guest*. Don't you see what this is, Gwen? It's personal. Sheila's calling me out! So my guest can't be just anyone!

GWEN. How about your best friend?

[MUSIC NO. 01C "THE YEAR OF THE WEDDINGS (PT. 3)"]

HENRY. Sorry. She's gotta be the soul-mate-y-est soulmate in the world. A refined, artsy, bohemian, earnest, sweet, sexy, smart, spiritual, best friend, nurturing, sophisticated, elegant lady!!

GWEN. OK, not to get your hopes up, but I was hanging at Starbucks the other day and struck up a conversation with someone I thought would be right for me but then realized was right for you.

HENRY. I can't marry a girl you met at Starbucks.

GWEN. Sure you can. Her name is Tamar and you came up.

HENRY. I did?

GWEN. I'm your best friend, remember? She's in PR which means she likes creative types. And get this: she thinks the Beatles' best song...of all time...is "Glass Onion."

HENRY. Now she sounds interesting. Tamar...

GWEN. Henry!

HENRY. *(Ruminating.)* Mrs. Tamar Mann...

GWEN. Henry, one step at a time!

HENRY.

THIS COULD BE THE YEAR OF MY WEDDING
A WEDDING OF MY OWN
I HANG BY A THREAD
'CAUSE I'M DESP'RATE TO WED
WHAT FUN IS LIFE ALONE?

GWEN. Right!

HENRY.

OH

HENRY & GWEN.

WHY NOT THE YEAR OF MY/YOUR WEDDING?

*(**GWEN** dials Tamar's number on Henry's cell.)*

THE DATE IS OVERDUE

HENRY.

MY BEST PLAN

*(***GWEN** *hands* **HENRY** *the phone.)*

MY BEST MAN

Hey Tamar, this is Henry – yeah, that's right, Gwen's friend. Yeah, "Glass Onion," right? So listen, I was wondering –

(Pause.)

What's that? Unh-huh. Unh-huh. Unh-huh. OK, then. Bye.

(He hangs up. There is silence.)

GWEN. So...??

*(***HENRY** *frowns.)*

Oh, sorry, man...

HENRY. *(Suddenly jubilant.)*

OH, THIS IS THE YEAR OF MY WEDDING
THE GROOM IS COMING THROUGH
LET BELLS CHIME
IT'S MY TIME

GWEN. Wait, you have a date with Tamar?

HENRY.

I DO!

*(***SHEILA** *re-enters.)*

SHEILA.

I DO!

GWEN.

NOT ONE MORE WEDDING!

HENRY.

THE YEAR OF MY WEDDING!

[MUSIC NO. 01D "THE YEAR OF THE WEDDINGS – PLAYOFF"]

Scene Two

(**HENRY** *is pacing on the street before a doorway, talking to himself.*)

HENRY. You're good-looking. You're smart. Women love you. You're good-looking. You're smart. Women love you. You're good-looking. You're smart. Women...

(*He notices the audience.*)

You see that button on that doorway? That's Tamar's buzzer. Operation Soulmate has officially begun.

(*He paces again.*)

You're good-looking. You're smart. Women love you. You're good-looking. You're smart. Women love you.

(*Now really psyching himself up.*)

You de man! You de man! You de man! You de man! You de man! YOU DE MAAAANNNNN!

(*He presses the button. It buzzes.*)

TAMAR. (*Offstage.*) Hello?

HENRY. (*Pulls himself together. As suavely as possible.*) Hey there. It's me. Henry.

TAMAR. (*Offstage.*) Great. Be right down.

HENRY. (*To audience.*) Did you hear that? She likes me! Now all I have to do is follow Gwen's instructions.

(**GWEN** *appears briefly.*)

GWEN & HENRY. Keep it light. No matter how good this Tamar looks, how funny she is, how much she knows about politics, art, or Sondheim...

HENRY. I, Henry Mann, will not under any circumstances imagine our wedding, children, or future life together!

(**TAMAR** *enters. She's lovely and dressed very arsty/downtown.*)

TAMAR. Henry?

[MUSIC NO. 02 "SHE'S MY WIFE"]

HENRY. *(Overcome, to audience.)*
SHE'S MY WIFE!
SEE HOW BEAUTIFUL SHE IS!
HOW POISED, HOW WARM, HOW WITTY
(Flagellating himself.) No! No! Stop it! Stop it!

TAMAR. Henry?

HENRY. *(Recovering.)* What? What? Oh, Tamar. Hello! Great to meet you.

TAMAR. You, too. I hope you haven't been waiting long.

HENRY. No, no. Just got here. Took the subway to a subway to a tram to a bus and boom. Here I am.

> *(To audience.)*

OH, MY WIFE!
SHE'LL LIVE UP TO EV'RY DREAM
I'VE EVER HAD!

AND OUR WEDDING INVITATIONS
WILL BE DONE BY CARTIER IN TEN-POINT FONT
WE'LL HAVE A SALSA BAND,
A PASTA BAR,
CHATEAUBRIAND
HONEYMOON IN MAUI
THEN GET HULU ON DEMAND

WHEN SHE'S MY WIFE
A COUNTRY HOUSE I'LL BUILD FOR HER
WELL…SUPERVISE. AND
WHAT A LIFE
FIRST, I'LL RAVISH HER AND THEN REGROUT OUR TUB

SO WHY SQUANDER TIME IN DATING
WITH A JUSTICE OF THE PEACE OFFSTAGE WAITING?
WHY DELAY THE CHILDREN WE CAN BE CREATING?
SHE'S MY WIFE
MY BEAUTIFUL WIFE!

> *(They have reached a table. The date is in progress. They are both slightly tipsy and having fun, laughing.)*

TAMAR. Hey, that's great!

HENRY. Great? Are you insane? The novel was rejected by ten publishers!

TAMAR. So what? That happens all the time. You just need to find the right editor. Your agent says she wants you to revise it, right?

HENRY. Yeah, true...

TAMAR. So do it. You'll get a deal. But listen! Your musical on *The Great Gatsby* sounds great. Why not focus on that?

HENRY. Really? I haven't touched it since college. I've only written four songs.

TAMAR. Well, finish it. *Gatsby* is such a massive achievement.

HENRY. Yes, massive. Isn't the language beautiful?

TAMAR. I worship Fitzgerald.

HENRY. Me, too! I wrote this big choral number based on the final line of the book. "Boats Against the Current." You don't think that's too pretentious, do you?

TAMAR. Not at all! Sing it!

HENRY. Sing it? Here?

TAMAR. Yeah. *(Breathy.)* Sing. It.

HENRY. Oh, OK.

> *(Passionately.)*

> SO WE BEAT ON!
> BOATS AGAINST THE CURRENT
> BORNE BACK
> CEASELESSLY
> INTO THE PAST!

TAMAR. Oh, my god! Brilliant!

HENRY. *(To audience.)* Can you believe this? A downtown girl who appreciates everything about me I want appreciated. Who actually likes the fact that I'm a starving artist!

TAMAR. Most of the men I meet are bankers or lawyers. Are they dull or what? I love guys with the courage to explore their creative side.

HENRY. *(To audience.)* See?

TAMAR. Gwen was right.

HENRY. About what?

TAMAR. You're cute. What are you doing Sunday afternoon?

HENRY. Hanging out with you?

TAMAR. Hell yes. There's an exhibit in a gallery I like.

HENRY. *(To audience.)* Woah, artsy, too.

  (To **TAMAR.***)* OK, cool. I like galleries. And...I like you.

> *(They are about to kiss when* **TAMAR** *pulls away, very excited.)*

TAMAR. Hey, I had a thought! Didn't Gatsby always wear a pink suit? How about using that as your Act One finale?

HENRY. Yeah. Could work.

  MY PINK SUIT
  PINK SUIT
  THERE'S NO SUBSTITUTE
  FOR MY PINK SUIT!

  How's that?

TAMAR. I love it! Is it a burden to be so talented? Well, good night.

> *(She exits.)*

HENRY. *(To himself as he waves goodbye.)*

  MY PINK SUIT!
  IT'S A BEAUT!
  BUT NOTHING IS CUTER THAN...

  SHE'S MY WIFE
  SO ADVENTUROUS
  WE'LL HAVE GREAT SEX WHILE JUMPING OUT OF PLANES
  WHAT A LIFE!
  AND WE'LL EVEN BUY A TIMESHARE IN NEPAL...

  (To audience.) Amazing! So how do you top a perfect date? You write the perfect, charming four a.m. text.

  (Talking as he texts.) "Dearest Glass Onion. Your song is in my heart. Thanks for the great evening. Hugs and kisses, Gatsby."

HENRY. *(Sends text, then to audience.)* Perfect. Short, to the point. A masterpiece!

OH, LET HER BE THE ONE
NOT ANOTHER DRY-RUN
MAKE IT MY TURN NOW

THEY SAY MEN DON'T WANT TO MARRY
MEN DON'T WANT TO SETTLE DOWN
BUT A MAN CAN SURE GET LONELY
AS THE ONLY SINGLE GUY IN TOWN!

(He hears a bring!)

Oh, my god! That has to be her! It has to be, right?

TAMAR. *(Offstage.)* Hey there. I just got your note and it was so sweet...which makes what I'm about to write even harder.

HENRY.

SHE'S MY W– WHAT??

TAMAR. *(Offstage.)* I don't know how else to say this but to say it. I'm just getting out of a relationship with Robert...

HENRY. Robert?

TAMAR. *(Offstage.)* And it occurs to me that I'm not ready to get involved with someone new. Especially now that I've met Cindy.

HENRY. Cindy?!

TAMAR. *(Offstage.)* I don't want to lead you on, right? Don't forget "My Pink Suit." It could be a showstopper. All Best, Tamar.

HENRY.

YOU'RE GOOD-LOOKING. YOU'RE SMART. WOMEN LOVE
YOU. YOU'RE GOOD-LOOKING. YOU'RE SMART

(Running out of steam.)

WOMEN...LOVE...YOU...

SHE'S MY OWN DAISY BUCHANAN
BUT SHE'LL NEVER LET A MAN LIKE HENRY MANN IN
SHE'S MY WIFE
MY *EX*-WIFE!

Scene Three

(**HENRY** *is asleep in his clothes, on his couch.
The landline rings.*)

HENRY. *(Sleepily.)* Yeah...? Hello?

[MUSIC NO. 02A "OBSCENE PHONE CALL #1"]

WOMAN'S VOICE.
I WANNA DO YOU ON THE DINING ROOM TABLE!

HENRY. Come again?

WOMAN'S VOICE.
I WANNA DO YOU ON THE DINING ROOM TABLE!

HENRY. Ah, you must want Gwen. She's still asleep.

(To audience.) The downside of living with a newly
single woman. Gwen moved in here about four months
ago after separating from her wife, Diana, this sweet
lady she met online. Ever since the breakup she's
worked through her pain by hooking up with half the
women on the Eastern Seaboard.

GWEN. *(Entering groggily.)* Was that for me?

HENRY. I have a feeling she'll call back.

GWEN. Yep. It seems to work that way. So how was your
night?

HENRY. Way romantic. Just me, her, and the memory of her
ex-boyfriend.

GWEN. Ouch.

HENRY. And Cindy!

GWEN. Cindy? How did I miss that? OK, well, if you're that
desperate to find the future Mrs. Mann, why don't you
finally ask out the girl in the apartment across the way?

HENRY. Yoga girl?

[MUSIC NO. 02B "SHE'S MY WIFE (YOGA GIRL)"]

(**GWEN** *and* **HENRY** *look on as she changes
to more humorously difficult and sexual
positions.*)

GWEN & HENRY. Ooh.

Ooh!

OOH.

GWEN. You'll never make me believe she has actual bones. Whatever, I've got to work.

(*She begins to exit, then turns.*)

Hey, Diana hasn't called, has she?

HENRY. (*To audience.*) I feel for Gwen. She's hurting. Then again, it serves her right. She did cheat on Diana.

GWEN. I can't believe she hasn't been in touch – not even once! What's that about?

HENRY. Women...

GWEN. Whatever. I'm going to spend some time with my script.

HENRY. Ah, *The Evolutionary Zygote*. How're rehearsals coming anyway?

GWEN. Good. As long as I get down all of my lines before next weekend.

HENRY. All your lines? You wrote the thing. You play a giant amoeba.

GWEN. A *talking* amoeba, dude. Who knows a shitload about Darwin. There's a lot to memorize.

(*The phone rings again.*)

HENRY. Oh, my god! (*Picks up the phone.*) Is this the new hip thing? Calling before eight in the morning on a weekend?

(*Lights up on* **CHRISTINE.** *Perhaps her nose is a bit crooked. Perhaps she has a slight unibrow. It doesn't matter. She has a down-to-earth attractiveness that some guys might overlook at first, then regret later.*)

CHRISTINE. Oh, my gosh. I woke you. You were asleep, right? And now you're up. Darnit! Go back to sleep, OK?

HENRY. Wait! Who is this?

CHRISTINE. Oh, it's Christine Warriner. From work.

GWEN. Who is it?

HENRY. *(For* **GWEN***'s benefit.)* Oh, hi *Christine*. What's going on?

CHRISTINE. You sure it's not too early?

HENRY. No, no. I'm up.

CHRISTINE. Well, listen. Remember I said I'm finishing up my student teaching? Anyway, Gwen mentioned you wrote some really clever kids' poems for your niece.

HENRY. Oh, Gwen said that?

CHRISTINE. So I wanted to know if you'd be willing to come in to P.S. 7 – that's where I'm a student teacher, P.S. 7 – and read to my kids. Oh, god. I so woke you. Shit! Just think about coming to my class, OK? They're third-graders and super cute. Find me at work this week.

HENRY. Wait, Christine. I really don't think my poems are... *(Realizes that she's hung up.)* Ready for popular consumption...

GWEN. *(As* **HENRY** *hangs up.)* Christine Warriner! My god! Why didn't I think of it. Forget yoga girl and everyone else. That's the girl you need to date! She's a rarity in this city: interesting but not insane!

[MUSIC NO. 02C "ALBRIGHT, PINKHAM & SCHWARTZ"]

(As **HENRY** *speaks, a law office with a small Xerox machine takes shape behind him.)*

HENRY. *(To audience.)* Gwen didn't let it go all weekend. She went right on about it until Monday night. You see, along with being roommates, Gwen and I work together, too – doing legal assistant work at Albright, Pinkham & Schwartz. Not that Gwen or I wanted to be lawyers. No, Albright employs a whole staff of writers, actors, grad students – even aspiring teachers like Christine – to work at night, all of us trying to make a buck to support our real careers.

GWEN. *(Proofreading quickly.)* Provided, however, that the company defined is owned by a third party who once knew a fourth party who liked to par-tay...oh, the hell with it! How can I concentrate on proofreading with Christine Warriner on the loose? The minute she walks into this room, I'm going to make it happen for you.

HENRY. The minute she walks into this room you will sit there and do nothing, get it? Now shut up about Christine, OK? She's probably too earnest for me anyway.

GWEN. Earnest? Wasn't that one of the things you wanted? Earnest, fun and kind?

HENRY. Listen, just be quiet about Christine, OK? I don't want to ask out Christine. I don't know if I even...oh, hi Christine!

>   (**CHRISTINE** *has entered carrying a giant load of documents, which she drops on the Xerox machine.*)

CHRISTINE. Hi. Listen, sorry about calling Saturday morning. I really shouldn't have –

HENRY. No, no, it's just that...my poems are terrible. Unadulterated pieces of garbage.

CHRISTINE. OK! Well...guess I gotta make some copies.

>   (*She gets to work.*)

GWEN. (*Looking up from the document, without missing a beat.*) I told you, she likes you. And you know what's better. It's her. The one who Xeroxed her ass and hung it in the supervisor's office.

HENRY. No. It can't be her. Christine teaches third grade.

GWEN. So a third grade teacher can't have a nice butt? Or want to share it with the world? Like I've been saying, this is the girl you should ask out.

HENRY. All right already! To tell the truth, I was going to – once.

GWEN. And?

HENRY. Look close. Right between her eyebrows.

GWEN. Yeah? So?

HENRY. Don't you see it?

GWEN. What?

HENRY. Man, don't pretend it's not there. The unibrow!

GWEN. I don't see anything.

HENRY. Look closer! It's sprouting over the bridge of her nose like a wild tuft of grass poking through a crack in the sidewalk! Life finds a way.

GWEN. That's why you didn't ask her out? Come on, Henry. This isn't about a little unibrow. You're still hurting over Sheila.

HENRY. *(Aside.)* That's the trouble with having a best friend. They know you too well.

> (**GWEN** *reaches into* **HENRY**'s *pocket and pulls out a piece of paper and approaches* **CHRISTINE**, *speaking loudly for her benefit.*)

GWEN. So this is your latest poem, Henry? *The Tale of the Otter*?

HENRY. Shut up! What are you doing?

GWEN. Helping you finally get a girl.

HENRY. How'd you get that?

GWEN. I stole it. *(Reading grandly.)* There once was an otter / named Benjamin Potter, who...

CHRISTINE. What was that?

GWEN. One of Henry's poems. Like I told you, the guy has written an entire collection for his niece, Jill.

CHRISTINE. You told me. That's sweet.

GWEN. Isn't it? Wanna hear it? We need an expert opinion.

HENRY. Gwen!

CHRISTINE. Why not?

> (**GWEN** *gives the poem to* **HENRY**.)

GWEN. Do the honors, my man.

[MUSIC NO. 03 "THE TALE OF THE OTTER"]

HENRY. It's not really finished.

CHRISTINE. That's OK.

HENRY. It's about an otter.

CHRISTINE. I heard.

HENRY. It's just a draft.

GWEN. Stop apologizing. Read.

HENRY.

> THERE ONCE WAS AN OTTER
> NAMED BENJAMIN POTTER
> WHO HAD QUITE A CRUSH ON THE ZOOKEEPER'S
> DAUGHTER
>
> THE ZOOKEEPER'S DAUGHTER
> WALKED BY THE WATER
> EACH MORNING AT TEN WITH A MILLIONAIRE YACHTER

> Oh, god. This so sucks.

CHRISTINE. No, it's cute.

> *(She takes the poem.)*

> THE MILLIONAIRE YACHTER,
> JOHN WITHERSPOON KOTTER,
> SPOTTED THE OTTER ADMIRING THE DAUGHTER

HENRY & CHRISTINE.

> THEN WITHERSPOON KOTTER
> GOT HOTTER AND HOTTER

HENRY.

> AND AIMED A SMALL ROCK AT THE DEWEY-EYED OTTER

> Well...

> THE ZOOKEEPER'S DAUGHTER
> CRIED OUT:

CHRISTINE.

> "YOU ROTTER
> HOW DARE YOU ASSAULT MR. BENJAMIN POTTER!"

HENRY.

> AND THAT'S WHEN THE OTTER

CHRISTINE.

> (THAT QUICK-THINKING PLOTTER)

HENRY & CHRISTINE.

> CRIED TO THE DAUGHTER: "WED ME, YOU OUGHT'ER!"

CHRISTINE.
>THE ZOOKEEPER'S DAUGHTER
>SPIED THE OTTER THAT SOUGHT HER
>AND THOUGHT TO HERSELF:

HENRY.
>"WHY NOT TIE THE KNOTTER?"
>"GOODBYE, MR. KOTTER!"

CHRISTINE.
>"I'LL BECOME MRS. POTTER!"

HENRY & CHRISTINE.
>AND LATER THAT DAY THEY WED UNDERWATER

HENRY.
>SO ENDS THE TALE OF HOW
>BENJAMIN POTTER

CHRISTINE.
>A LOVABLE OTTER

HENRY.
>DEFEATED A YACHTER

HENRY & CHRISTINE.
>PURSUING A DAUGHTER
>AND FINALLY GOT HER!

>>(**HENRY** *and* **CHRISTINE** *look at each other,*
>>*enamored and speechless.* **GWEN** *jumps in.*)

GWEN. So here's the thing. Henry is free Friday night and would love to take you out. Sound good?

CHRISTINE. Uh, yeah. OK.

GWEN. He'll pick you up when?

CHRISTINE. How's eight?

GWEN. Eight it is. Any food allergies?

CHRISTINE. No.

GWEN. Perfect. He'll see you then.

CHRISTINE. OK, fun. Bye.

GWEN. Bye!

HENRY. Bye!
>(*To* **GWEN** *as* **CHRISTINE** *exits.*) Idiot.

GWEN. Do me a favor.

HENRY. What?

GWEN. Don't blow this one.

Scene Four

[MUSIC NO. 03A "ORBITING IN YOUR UNIVERSE"]

(The scene shifts fluidly to the Lookout, a rotating restaurant in the heart of Times Square.)

VOICE-OVER. Welcome to the Lookout, friends, in the heart of Times Square. Just a reminder: if you opted for our all-you-can-eat salad bar we've recently added...capers!

> *(**HENRY** and **CHRISTINE** enter, dressed for their date. A cheesy lounge singer appears, **HARVEY TRITONE**.)*

TRITONE. *(Singing to the patrons, à la a bad Sinatra.)*
SOMETIMES LIFE CAN BE PERVERSE
ROMANTIC'LLY I WAS IN A HEARSE
NOW I'M LOVESICK FOR YOU, PLEASE FIND A NURSE
'CAUSE I'M ORBITING IN YOUR U-NI-VERSE!

CHRISTINE. So this is the famous rotating restaurant.

HENRY. Right. So cheesy it's chic. See New York's grandest sights while enjoying the worst band and buffet this side of Jersey.

CHRISTINE. I love it.

HENRY. *(As **CHRISTINE** walks to a table.)* I've got to hand it to Gwen. Over dinner Christine and I bonded about practically everything. She even agreed to come here, my favorite stupid-hangout in the city: a slab of suburbia plopped down in the middle of Manhattan.

TRITONE.
SMITTEN BY A LOVELY CURSE
I'VE CAUGHT A VIBE I CAN'T REVERSE
NO OTHER CHICKS WILL I COERCE
WHILE I'M ORBITING IN YOUR UN-I-*BROW*!

> *(**HENRY** is shocked and mouths to the audience, "Did you hear that?" **CHRISTINE** and **HENRY** don't know what to say. Then they both speak at once, quickly, to break the tension.)*

HENRY.	**CHRISTINE.**
So you said you used to play basketball in high school?	By the way, I really do think my kids would love your poems. They really are great.

(Another beat. Which conversation to pursue?)

HENRY. Thanks. I mean, about the poems.

CHRISTINE. You know, I write, too. These super obvious folk-songy guitar tunes. You'd probably puke.

HENRY. Puke? No, I love super obvious folk-songy guitar tunes.

CHRISTINE. I am probably a better basketball player than songwriter, though.

HENRY. My niece Jill and I play in the park sometimes... *(He takes a risk.)* We should play sometime. A little one-on-one.

CHRISTINE. I was All-State, you know.

HENRY. So you'll win.

CHRISTINE. I like a guy who isn't scared of losing to a girl. But hey, isn't Gwen in some performance art thing she wrote? We could go to that.

HENRY. Well, if you really want. It's a one-man show where Gwen plays an amoeba who lectures at Harvard.

CHRISTINE. Sounds very Off-Off Broadway. But I guess it could be fun, right?

HENRY. Well, why not? I'll double-check with Gwen about an extra ticket. If you can believe it, the thing's sold out. It's tomorrow night.

CHRISTINE. I think I have this weird dinner-movie-karaoke thing with my cousin and some of her friends. But I bet I can get out of it.

HENRY. I'll call you tomorrow to confirm?

CHRISTINE. Cool! So it's another date!

[MUSIC NO. 04 "HARD"]

Oh, wow. I sort of like this song.

HENRY. Oh? You do?

> *(An awkward beat.* **CHRISTINE** *is waiting for* **HENRY** *to ask her to dance.)*

CHRISTINE. So...do you wanna...you know...?

HENRY. Sure. Why not?

> *(***HENRY*** *and* ***CHRISTINE*** *stand, then embrace awkwardly.)*

OH, GOD
WHY DID YOU GIVE ME TWO LEFT FEET
AND NEITHER ONE CAN KEEP A BEAT?
WHY IS THIS...HARD?

OH, GREAT
A FIRST DATE SLOW DANCE FAR TOO SOON
WHY DON'T THEY PLAY A FASTER TUNE?
DANCING'S SO HARD

SEE HER TILTED GRIN
SLIGHTLY OUT OF LINE
IMPERFECTLY DIVINE

BUT NEVERMIND HER FACE
FOCUS ON THE CHASE
HER EMBRACE...

OH, YES
I FEEL HER UNDULATING HIPS
A WARM BREATH STIRRING FROM HER LIPS
COULD I BE...HARD?!

OH, NO
HER BREASTS ARE PRESSED AGAINST MY CHEST
I'M DON QUIXOTE ON A QUEST
THAT'S OH SO...HARD

WHY IS SHE KEEPING MUM?
IF SHE CANNOT TELL, SHE'S NUMB
SHOULD I TAKE IT AS A CUE?
WHISPER, "BABE, THIS ONE'S FOR YOU"

I AM MORTIFIED
HELL, JUST ENJOY THE RIDE

SHE PLACES ME AT EASE...
WELL, ABOVE THE WAIST, BELOW THE KNEES
THE REST IS...

CHRISTINE.

NICE
DANCING TOGETHER IN THE DARK
I THINK I MAY HAVE DRAWN A SPARK
THIS BOY IS...

HENRY.

DOES SHE KNOW I'M VERY HARD?

CHRISTINE.

OK,
DO I PRETEND IT'S THERE AT ALL
WHAT IS THE PROTOCOL?
THE SITUATION'S HARD

HENRY.

PRETEND MY PHONE'S ON VIBRATE

CHRISTINE.

SHOULD I PLAY IT SLY?
NOT SINCE JUNIOR HIGH
HAVE I ATTRACTED SUCH ATTENTION

CHRISTINE.   **HENRY.**

COULD HE BE THE ONE?   COULD SHE BE THE ONE?

HENRY.

IT'S A LOADED GUN

HENRY & CHRISTINE.

AN UNEXPECTED INTERVENTION

CHRISTINE.

THANK GOD, THE SONG IS COMING TO AN END

HENRY.

WILL SHE MEND OR IS SHE PERMANENTLY SCARRED?

HENRY & CHRISTINE.

THE AGONY
THE ECSTASY

CHRISTINE.

TO MAKE A REAL CONNECTION

HENRY.

TO NO LONGER FEAR REJECTION

CHRISTINE.

TO MEET A NORMAL GUY

HENRY.

A GIRL TO LOVE UNTIL I DIE IS

HENRY & CHRISTINE.

HARD, SO HARD

REAL HARD, HARD

HENRY. Oh, what the hell.

(He kisses her.)

Scene Five

[MUSIC NO. 04A "OBSCENE PHONE CALL #2"]

HENRY. As you can see, Christine and I hit it off. So when I get home, I go on Facebook to look at her page.
(He looks at the page, then to audience.) Very nice! So I call Gwen to ask about tickets for the following night.
(Into the phone to Gwen.) It was great. After the date we made out on her front stoop for twenty-two and a half minutes.

> *(A beat.)*

Yeah, I timed it.

> *(GWEN appears to the side, on the phone.)*

GWEN. Wow. Impressive.

HENRY. Anyway, so we want to see your show tomorrow night. Can I get an extra ticket?

GWEN. Sure, I can hook you up.

HENRY. Great, thanks.

GWEN. Listen, Henry. I've really got to go.

HENRY. Yeah, I get it. Have fun with the girls.

> *(He hangs up. GWEN makes a call.)*

GWEN. Hey, Diana. Yeah, yeah, it's me again. Man, I am so hoping to reach an actual person one of these days. Just give me a call whenever you get the chance.

> *(Lights cut back to HENRY. The landline rings immediately.)*

HENRY. *(Answering.)* Yeah?

WOMAN'S VOICE.
    I WANNA DO YOU ON THE DINING ROOM TABLE!

HENRY. She's out! Damn. We've got to get rid of this landline.

> *(He slams down the phone. It rings again. He answers, exasperated.)*

Yeah, I wanna do you on the dining room table, too!

> (**MRS. MANN**, *Henry's mother, well-meaning but comically aggressive, appears on the other side of the stage, holding a phone.*)

MRS. MANN. Henny, honey!

HENRY. Not a good time, Mom! Why are you calling at midnight?

MRS. MANN. I saw you were on Facebook.

HENRY. Can't you at least call my cell for a change?

MRS. MANN. What? And give you cancer? Now how was the teacher?

HENRY. She was fine, Mom.

MRS. MANN. That's all? Fine? You can share with me, Henny. I'm a therapist now.

HENRY. You have one patient. Your cleaning woman!

MRS. MANN. Well, I'm glad to see that you're finally over Sheila. I was worried about you.

HENRY. Oh, why'd you have to mention Sheila?

> (**MRS. MANN** *exits and* **SHEILA** *appears.* **HENRY** *is aghast.*)

SHEILA. Having troubles, Henry? Because perhaps I can help.

> (**HENRY** *clicks off the phone.*)

HENRY. Oh, god! Dream Sheila! She's behind me, isn't she? Go!

SHEILA. You know you can't control that overly active imagination of yours, Henry. But since I'm here, I want to say how badly I feel about how things ended between us.

HENRY. Which time are you referring to? When you dumped me senior week or when I proposed last year?

SHEILA. I guess both. But you've got to admit that it was the right move. You're wonderful Henry but we're so different it's stunning. Thor wears Brooks Brothers, you wear L.L.Bean. Thor and I are moving to Greenwich. You'd rather be dead.

HENRY. True – but I should've dumped *you* first! You could never appreciate an artist.

SHEILA. *(Gently.)* A *starving* artist. But I want us to remain friends. That's why I invited you to the wedding.

HENRY. You didn't do it to shove your happiness down my throat? Because that's sort of what it feels like.

SHEILA. Henry, you were the most important person in my life for over five years. In a way you're still the person who knows me best. Better even than Thor. My soulmate.

    (The word "soulmate" echoes humorously.)

HENRY. Ah, that word again. Stop.

SHEILA. What word?

    (Echoing weirdly.) Soulmate!

      *(**HENRY** recoils in pain.)*

Soulmate? SOULMATE?

HENRY. *(Recovering.)* Shut up! I have my own soulmate now! Christine Warriner! You and I were never meant to be. Christine and I are going to do it our way. The New York City way!

[MUSIC NO. 05 "SETTLING DOWN"]

We aren't going to fester in some sorry semblance of a life in the 'burbs!

LIFE WITH CHRISTINE –
SAFE AND SECURE
UNSURPRISING BUT NOT UNINSPIRED
NO MORTGAGE TO PAY
NO CAR TO INSURE
JUST US, NO ASSEMBLY REQUIRED

OH, I'M SETTLING DOWN
LEAVING BEHIND MY OLD SINGLE LIFE
NO MORE BAD DATES ON A SATURDAY NIGHT
WOND'RING IF THIS ONE WILL FIN'LLY BE RIGHT

LISTEN UP, SHEILA, I'VE FOUND MY GREEN LIGHT
SHE'S CHRISTINE
MY TRIPLE CROWN

HENRY.	**SHEILA.**
YEAH, I'M SETTLING	YEAH, YOU'RE SETTLING

HENRY.

DOWN.

In fact, I'm going to confirm tomorrow night right now.

(He reaches for the phone. He goes to dial.)

SHEILA. Go ahead. What's stopping you?

*(**HENRY** hesitates.)*

HENRY. Shush!

I'LL NEVER TRADE
MY HEART FOR DÉCOR
NEVER LIVE THAT KIND OF LIE

I'LL CHOOSE CHRISTINE
WHO'LL FEED MY SOUL MORE
THAN ANYTHING GOOGLE COULD BUY

HENRY.	**SHEILA.**
YES, I'M SETTLING DOWN	SETTLING DOWN

HENRY.

SETTLING IN, AND I'M SET FOR LIFE
CHRISTINE IS A TEACHER, SHE'LL MAKE A GREAT MOM
NO MATTER THE CHALLENGE, SHE'LL ALWAYS STAY CALM

SHEILA.

WITH "GREEN EGGS AND HAM" AND THE TWENTY-THIRD
PSALM
SHE'LL ERASE ANY FROWN

*(**GWEN** enters.)*

HENRY.	**SHEILA.**
YEAH, I'M SETTLING DOWN!	YEAH, YOU'RE SETTLING DOWN!

SHEILA. So call her why don't you. She is your soulmate, isn't she?

HENRY.

A SOULMATE?

IT'S COMPLETELY INSANE

DOES SUCH A THING EVEN EXIST?

IS IT POSSIBLE TO FIND LOVE TO

    OUTLAST THE HEAVENS?

SHEILA & GWEN.

AH OO

AH OO

AH

> (**GWEN** *appears on the other side of the stage, drinking alone at a bar.*)

HENRY, SHEILA & GWEN.

ONE LOUSY SOULMATE!

HENRY.

AM I MOVING TOO FAST?

IS THERE SOMEONE I MIGHT'VE MISSED?

CAN CHRISTINE BE THE ONE?

GWEN.

WAS DIANA THE ONE?

GWEN.   **HENRY.**

WAS SHE MY HOMERUN?   IS SHE MY HOMERUN?

SHEILA.

HOW CAN I IGNORE THOR?

> (**HENRY** *picks up the phone, poised to dial.*)

HENRY.

OH, I'M SETTLING DOWN

BUT IS SETTLING FALLING INTO AN ABYSS?

CHRISTINE'S A NICE GIRL, I ADMIT WE HAD FUN

BUT THAT DOESN'T MEAN SHE IS SECOND TO NONE

I'M THINKING MY SEARCH HAS JUST BARELY BEGUN

GONNA SCOUR THIS TOWN

HENRY.

THERE'S A WORLD FULL

    OF LOVE TO EXPLORE

SO HELL, IS IT WRONG TO

    WANT MORE?

INSTEAD OF JUST

    SETTLING FOR

SETTLING DOWN!

SHEILA & GWEN.

OOO

LOVE TO EXPLORE

FIND SOMETHING MORE

INSTEAD

GWEN & SHEILA.

DOWN, DOWN, DOWN, DOWN, DOWN!

SETTLING DOWN!

(**HENRY** *dramatically pockets his phone on the button.*)

[MUSIC NO. 05A "THE EVOLUTIONARY ZYGOTE"]

Scene Six

(Lights up on **GWEN**, *onstage and in character. She emotes very dramatically. This is over-the-top, very bad performance art.)*

GWEN. How can we adapt when we're only zygotes...at a cocktail party...swimming in a sea of lost connections.

(She bows, accepting thunderous applause. Lights up on **HENRY** *in a neighborhood bar.)*

HENRY. Yep. I have to stomach two and half hours of *that*. And to make matters worse, afterwards I have to listen to people shower Gwen with compliments. Right! *Compliments?* I'm about to make an excuse to leave, when who walks in...?

(Enter **TAMAR.***)*

TAMAR. Henry?

HENRY. *(To audience.)* Tamar. Then she said the perfect thing.

TAMAR. God, that show SUCKED!

HENRY. Yes! Thank you. I mean, I love Gwen, and I feel terrible about ragging on her work. Maybe I'm just jealous, I don't know, but really. It was bad, right? And everyone loved it.

TAMAR. They're either pretentious or being nice. I sat there thinking how your Gatsby is going to be so so SO much better.

HENRY. No fooling? You did? Because to tell the truth, this whole thing sort of made me nervous. I mean, if this is what people like...

TAMAR. Not sane people, don't worry. How'd your finale go again?

(Sings passionately, she remembers it.)

SO WE BEAT ON
BOATS AGAINST THE CURRENT...

HENRY & TAMAR.

 BORNE BACK CEASELESSLY INTO THE PAST!

HENRY. Wow, you really liked it, huh?

TAMAR. No...I loved it! But you know, I was thinking... You might be able to learn something from Gwen. Her show was terrible, but it did take risks.

HENRY. Is this your thing? You blow off guys by text then criticize their writing?

TAMAR. Hey, don't producers like things that are edgy?

HENRY. So what? I should make Gatsby a finger puppet?

TAMAR. Well, no. But Bernstein and Sondheim could've written a musical version of *Romeo and Juliet*. Instead, they set it on the West Side. Think outside the box.

HENRY. Sondheim. Cool. OK, anything else?

TAMAR. Yeah. I didn't come here to see a show about a deranged amoeba. I came to see you. What would you say if I told you that when we went on our date, I wasn't as available as I should have been. But that now I am.

HENRY. I'd say, why did you go on the date at all?

TAMAR. Good question. But then I'd say, I know that I probably shouldn't have, but now I'm glad that I did.

HENRY. Then *I'd* say, the last thing I need is a rebound.

TAMAR. Yeah, but here's the thing. Technically I'm out of rebound mode. I didn't tell you but Robert is married. Lives in Great Neck. Three kids. Stupid, huh? And Cindy? Well, let's just say we're moving in opposite directions.

HENRY. Meaning...?

TAMAR. I wouldn't blame you for hating me, Henry, but I really do like you. You're funny and sweet and creative. My shrink says I'm ready to be involved with a nice human. So does my masseuse! Oh, god! I haven't been able to stop thinking about you all week!

HENRY. *(To audience.)* I chewed on it...

 FOR TWO WHOLE SECONDS!

> *(He pounces on* **TAMAR**. *They make out passionately, ripping off each other's clothes.)*

[MUSIC NO. 05B "SHE'S MY WIFE – REPRISE"]

HENRY. *(To audience as* **TAMAR** *gropes him.)* Don't judge me. Don't forget. Tamar was the one I liked first. She's got it all! Besides, a guy like me needs a muse. Tamar'll push me to be a better writer.

SHE'S MY WIFE!

> *(***TAMAR** *pulls* **HENRY** *offstage.* **HENRY** *returns a second later to address the audience.)*

I didn't leave her apartment for twenty-three hours and fourteen minutes. *(He looks at his Fitbit.)* It wasn't until my 560th step on the walk home the next day that I remembered Christine. I really should've called her. Then again, we only said we'd be in touch. For all I know, she might have woken up and decided it was all a big mistake. It's possible. No, Christine probably wouldn't even care if she heard from me again. It was only a first date, right?

[MUSIC NO. 06 "IT'S ONLY A FIRST DATE"]

> *(The lights come up on* **CHRISTINE**.*)*

CHRISTINE.
MAYBE YOU WILL NEVER KNOW HIS FAV'RITE BAND AT
    WOODSTOCK
HIS FAV'RITE FILM BY HITCHCOCK
THE BOOKS HE'S READ, HIS TOUCH IN BED
YOU MAY NEVER WAKE UP TO HIS HOMEMADE CHEESE
    FRITTATA
THERE'S NOT A LOT OF THINGS YOU CAN CLAIM...

'CAUSE IT'S ONLY A FIRST DATE
IT'S FAR FROM A LIFETIME
NO INVESTMENT...SO THERE'S NO RETURN
YOU CAN LAUGH AT HIS JOKES
BUT YOU WON'T MEET HIS FOLKS
'CAUSE IT'S ONLY A FIRST DATE...

MAYBE WE WILL NEVER RIDE THE RAPIDS IN A KAYAK
OR BICYCLE THROUGH NYACK
SHARE A VIEW
A NETFLIX QUEUE
MAYBE WE WILL NEVER GET TO SEE WHO WINS AT PING
 PONG
OR SOMEDAY HAVE A SONG OF OUR OWN...

'CAUSE IT'S ONLY A FIRST DATE
A FEW HOURS THAT FLEW BY
THOUGH IT FELT AS IF THERE MIGHT BE MORE TO COME
NO REAL MEMORIES SHARED
DON'T PRETEND THAT HE CARED...

DON'T BE FOOLED BY THE STARS THAT LIT THE SKY
OR WAS IT THE LIGHT IN HIS EYES?
BY NOW IT SHOULD COME AS NO SURPRISE
THAT LIFE DOESN'T GO AS PLANNED
STILL, IT WAS GOOD TO HOLD HIS HAND...

AND MAYBE YOU'LL FORGET HOW REASSURING WERE HIS
 KISSES
IT'S EASY TO DISMISS THE WHOLE NIGHT...
'CAUSE IT'S ONLY AN HORS D'OEUVRE
IT'S HARDLY AN ENTRÉE
BUT IT KIND OF DULLS THE HUNGER FOR A WHILE
YOU'LL FORGET BY NEXT WEEK
BUT REMEMBER HIS SMILE...

FOR IT'S ONLY A DANCE
IT'S ONLY A MEAL
IT'S ONLY A GUY
SO COME ON, GET REAL
THERE'S NO CHANCE IN HELL
THAT HE FEELS WHAT YOU FEEL...

'CAUSE IT'S ONLY A FIRST DATE
NOTHING MORE

Scene Seven

[MUSIC NO. 07 "WHAT'S THE MATTER WITH HENRY?"]

(**GWEN** *is playing hoops.* **HENRY** *enters as she sings.*)

GWEN.

WHAT'S THE MATTER WITH HENRY?
HE'S STRANGELY FULL OF PEP
HAVE YOU SEEN MY BUDDY HENRY?
THERE'S A SHUFFLE IN HIS STEP

WHEREVER YOU LOOK
HE'S WITH TAMAR
IN EV'RY NOOK
GUESS WHAT?
TAMAR

(*She exits.*)

HENRY.

I'M OFF THE HOOK
ALL FOR A LADY NAMED TAMAR
SO SHE'S GOT A PAST THAT'S SORT OF BLEAK
AND VISITS HER SHRINK
THREE TIMES A WEEK
SHE IS MY LIFE
MY CPR
MY TAMAR!

(*His landline rings. He sees the caller ID.*)

Hi Mom.

(**MRS. MANN** *appears.*)

MRS. MANN. Henny, honey! How did it go with the teacher?

HENRY. She was nice, Mom. But this one gets me. Tamar.

MRS. MANN. You mean you didn't call the teacher?

HENRY. Well, I was going to but then I didn't. I mean, we only had one date.

MRS. MANN.

SPARE ME YOUR B.S., HENRY
GET YOUR BUTT OFF THE BENCH
YOU'VE HAD YOUR SPREE
NOW WHAT'LL YOU BE:
A LOSER OR A MENSCH?
TELL HER YOU'RE TAKEN OR CRAZY
TELL HER YOU MIGHT BE SECRETLY GAY
BUT DO IT, HENRY!
THEN SEND A LOVELY BOUQUET

Roses work. Also tulips.

(**MRS. MANN** *exits.*)

HENRY. OK, OK, I will.

(To audience.) I didn't. Again, I wanted to but my mind
was sort of elsewhere.

SHE SAID...

(**TAMAR** *pops her head out of the wings.*)

TAMAR.

I LOVE YOU!

(**GWEN** *enters.*)

GWEN.

THIS IS PRETTY QUICK

TAMAR.

LOVEY DOVE YOU

GWEN.

I THINK I MAY BE SICK

HENRY.

HAVE I MENTIONED THAT I LOVE HER, TOO?

GWEN.

YOU MIGHT HAVE SAID

HENRY.

SHE SAID SHE LOVES ME!
IS PART OF ME!
THEN SHE CALLED ME HER "LEETLE PEEGDOG"

GWEN. What?

HENRY.

AND I CALLED HER "MY FLUFFY MISS"

GWEN. Oh, god.

HENRY.

TO MARK OUR LOVE SHE GAVE ME THIS!

(He puts on an artsy hat.)

GWEN. I'm trying really hard to pretend that's not a beret.

HENRY. Shut up. It's a *chapeau.* It's important to cultivate a downtown writer bohemian image.

GWEN. Who said you needed a new image? You need someone who appreciates you as you are. A best friend.

HENRY. Come on. It doesn't work that way and you know it. I mean, was Diana your best friend?

GWEN. *(Hadn't thought of it before.)* Huh? Is Tamar yours?

HENRY. *(Not sure.)* Well?

(They ponder it and look at each other, then realize.)

GWEN & HENRY. You're my best friend!

HENRY. Wouldn't it be amazing? To be married to the person you want to watch a game with.

GWEN. Drink beer with.

HENRY. Why can't a wife be like...you!

(They hug.)

GWEN. Too bad this will never work.

HENRY. You think?

GWEN. I'm really hoping to work things out with Diana. If she'd ever answer my calls.

HENRY. For what it's worth, I'd answer your calls.

TAMAR. *(Entering.)* Henry!

GWEN. In the meantime, part of friendship is honesty. So if you want Tamar to be that best friend, tell her you need to lose the beret.

(She exits.)

TAMAR. Lose the chapeau?

HENRY. *(As he takes off the hat.)* Listen, Tamar. I do have a slightly oblong head that really may not be conducive to...

TAMAR.

> TAKE A DEEP BREATH, MY PEEGDOG
> YOU CAN'T ADMIT DEFEAT
>
> THE HAT'S NOT TOO MUCH
> HERE'S ANOTHER TOUCH
> TO MAKE YOUR LOOK COMPLETE

You need to step up your game. Especially now that you've decided to set your Gatsby in Havana!

HENRY. I have?

TAMAR.

> YOU NEED A DOSE OF KICK-ASS FUNK
> IF YOU WANNA MAKE GOOD ART
> YOU'RE A HAPPENING WRITER
> TIME TO LOOK THE PART

I set up an appointment with my stylist. I'm going to make this city light up every time your hot little feet touch the sidewalk.

> *(She blows him a kiss and leaves.)*

HENRY.

> WHEREVER I GO, I'LL HAVE TAMAR
> THE GUYS'LL ALL KNOW I'VE *HAD* TAMAR
> NOT EVEN VAN GOGH
> COULD PAINT A PICTURE AS HOT AS TAMAR

> *(He exits as **GWEN** enters, proofreading a document. **CHRISTINE** enters.)*

GWEN. Hey, Christine.

CHRISTINE. Hi. Interesting case?

GWEN. Who knows? Just because I proofread this stuff doesn't mean I understand it.

CHRISTINE. I know, right?

GWEN. Legalese is so confusing.

CHRISTINE. It's like run-on sentences have conspired to spawn even longer run-on sentences.

> (**HENRY** *enters with a hot new look, very downtown. He is very pleased with himself.* **GWEN** *and* **CHRISTINE** *are shocked.*)

GWEN. Oh, my god! Henry! What did you do to yourself?

HENRY. Shut up! I've never looked hotter!

CHRISTINE. Henry?

HENRY. Oh, hi Christine... *(Very fast.)* How good to see you! And listen, even though it was only one date, I realize now that protocol says I probably owed you a face-to-face breakup, and I really blew that one, so I'm sorry about that. You have a good heart, Christine. I mean, a great heart! With awesome ventricles. But you see, I met someone else and I'm rocking this cool new look. OK, then. God, I'm glad we talked.

> *(He exits.)*

CHRISTINE.
> WHAT'S THE MATTER WITH HENRY?

GWEN.
> IS HE IN LOVE?

CHRISTINE.
> OR JUST OUT OF STEP?

GWEN.
> THAT LOOK IS OBSCENE

CHRISTINE.
> HE'S A CROSS BETWEEN
> MY AUNT MARTHA AND JOHNNY DEPP
> I SHOULD HAVE KNOWN THAT A GUY LIKE HIM
> WOULD BE SLIM ON CLASS

> *(Calling into the wings.)*

> BY THE WAY, HENRY!
> THAT XEROX *WAS* MY ASS!

GWEN. I knew it! God, you're beautiful.

CHRISTINE. Thank you.

(CHRISTINE exits. GWEN sings with HENRY, who re-enters.)

GWEN.

WHAT'S THE MATTER WITH HENRY?

HENRY.

IS IT WRONG THAT I REFUSE TO FEEL CONTRITE?

GWEN.

SOMETHING'S THE MATTER WITH –

HENRY.

THERE'S NOTHING THE MATTER WITH HENRY
FOR ONCE, EV'RYTHING FEELS RIGHT

WHEREVER I LOOK, I SEE TAMAR!
NO LONGER A SHNOOK WITH MY TAMAR!
HELL, I'LL EVEN COOK
ALL FOR MY LADY NAMED TAMAR

TAMAR. I've got it! We'll produce a reading of your show!

GWEN. You think it's ready for that?

TAMAR. Henry will make it ready and I'll help organize it! I'm in PR, remember? We'll invite industry people! Producers!

HENRY. *The Green Light*, the musical!

TAMAR. This time next year, Broadway!

HENRY. Works for me!

GWEN. Don't get ahead of yourself, big guy.

HENRY. I know, Gwen! But come on, just be happy for me, OK?

GWEN. OK... Why not? Broadway!

(The trio is now outside, roaming the city.)

GWEN, HENRY & TAMAR.

WHAT'S THE MATTER WITH HENRY?
THIS DUDE IS WALKING THE WALK

GWEN.

NOTHING'S THE MATTER

HENRY.	**GWEN & TAMAR.**
WHEN MY SHOW IS A HIT	WOAH!

HENRY.

> SHEILA WILL WRIGGLE
> > AND SPIT
> LIKE A TROUT FLOPPING
> > ON A DOCK

GWEN & TAMAR.

> YEAH!

GWEN.

> CRAWLING OUT OF HIS CAVE

TAMAR.

> HE'S RIDING A WAVE

HENRY.

> NOW I'LL HAVE MYSELF A BALL

GWEN, HENRY & TAMAR.

> WHAT'S THE MATTER WITH HENRY?

HENRY. Hey, Tamar. How'd you like to go to my ex-almost-fiancée's wedding next month?

TAMAR. Sure. I'd love to!

GWEN, HENRY & TAMAR.

> NOTHING AT ALL!

Scene Eight

[MUSIC NO. 07A "SEGUE TO OFFICE COPIER"]

HENRY. The next couple of weeks rush by in a crazy blur. While I work like a madman on *The Green Light*, Tamar finds a great little space above a Toyota dealership on 11th Avenue. Before long, the reading is right around the corner and I'm making illegal copies of the programs at the law firm.

(He is now at the office. He rushes to the Xerox machine to make copies of his flier. **CHRISTINE** *enters at the same time to copy a flier of her own. They almost bump into each other.)*

Oh, hey...sorry, I didn't see you there.

CHRISTINE. Yeah. Well, that's OK.

(Each waits for the other to use the machine. Then they each reach for it at the same time, then pull back awkwardly.)

HENRY. You go first.

CHRISTINE. *(Starting to copy.)* So Henry... How are you?

HENRY. Fine, fine. I'm good. Real good. Nothing special going on at all. Just the normal stuff.

CHRISTINE. Oh really? But you're seeing someone, right?

HENRY. Yeah, it's good. Nice, you know? Just taking it slow, easing into it, seeing where it goes. So...uh, what have you got there?

CHRISTINE. Oh, me? Just a dumb flier about this thing I'm doing. Doesn't matter. What's that?

HENRY. Oh, this? A poster about a reading I'm putting together. Maybe you'd like to come? Oh, you're probably busy.

CHRISTINE. Yeah, I just started seeing someone, too. Someone from school.

HENRY. Hey, that's great. Good for you.

CHRISTINE. But you know, it's early.

HENRY. Yeah. Relationships are *hard*.

CHRISTINE. *(Painfully remembering their date.)* Uh, yeah...

> *(An extremely awkward beat. What can either of them possibly say?)*

HENRY. I mean, not *hard*. Complicated. Right, complicated.

CHRISTINE. Like they say, timing is everything, huh?

HENRY. Yeah. It is.

CHRISTINE. Well, good luck with your show.

> *(She exits.)*

HENRY. *(Calling after her.)* Yeah and good luck with that flier thing.

> *(To audience.)* Christine's right. Timing *is* everything. Maybe that's why Sheila rejected me. Twice.

SHEILA. *(Entering.)* I rejected you because in college your manic pursuit of everything was kind of adorable. But now, not so much.

HENRY. So I have a lot of interests. What's wrong with that?

SHEILA. Nothing. I can't wait to see what you'll be when you grow up. When you're ready to commit.

HENRY. But I *am* ready to commit! I'm writing my own show and guess what?

[MUSIC NO. 08 "THE RIGHT TIME TO PROPOSE"]

I'm taking Tamar to your wedding in one month – as my fiancée! Yes! Mrs. Tamar Mann! And this time I'll get it right!

> (**SHEILA** *exits as the scene shifts to a city street.*)

HOW DO YOU KNOW THE RIGHT TIME TO PROPOSE?
TELL ME, WHAT IS THE KEY?
IF TWO MONTHS HAVE PASSED
IS IT TOO FAST
TO GET DOWN ON ONE KNEE?

AND ONCE YOU'VE DECIDED TO ASK HER
WHAT IS THE BEST WAY TO STRIKE?
SOMETHING ROMANTIC
THAT ISN'T TOO FRANTIC
LIKE:

Got it! Smack in the middle of Times Square on the way to see *Hamilton*, premium seats, after springing for a full-blown, five-course meal!

WOMEN LIKE DINNER AND SHOWS
THAT'S THE RIGHT WAY TO PROPOSE

(TAMAR enters. HENRY takes her arm.)

TAMAR. That was such a delicious meal.

HENRY. That Bobby Flay's a genius.

TAMAR. You know, I haven't been able to stop humming your new Act Two song all day.

HOW I LOVE DR. ECKLEBURG'S EYES!

HENRY. That's great. Listen, Tamar...

TAMAR.

THOSE EYES!

HENRY. Tamar!

TAMAR.

THOSE ASTONISHING, ADMONISHING EYES...

(The wail of a siren fills the stage. HENRY has to shout over it. The NAKED COWBOY appears.)

HENRY. Listen, Tamar! I know we haven't known each other all that long! But I don't know! The gorgeous lights of Times Square are...

TAMAR. Oh, my god! I am so over that stupid naked cowboy. *(Shouts.)* No one cares! Put some clothes on!

HENRY. *(To audience.)* Maybe Times Square wasn't the best idea?

HOW DO YOU KNOW THE RIGHT TIME TO PROPOSE?
AND BE SURE IT'S NO WHIM?
WHAT ARE THE SIGNS
TO REHEARSE YOUR BEST LINES

AND GO OUT ON A LIMB?
YOU'VE GOT THE ICE IN YOUR POCKET
YOU TRY HARD NOT TO OBSESS
ON A ROLL, YOU CAN'T STOP IT
BUT WHERE SHOULD YOU POP IT?
AH, YES!

The easy way! The Sunday morning surprise. Tried and true!

DROP BY WITH SOME LOX AND A ROSE
THAT'S THE RIGHT WAY TO PROPOSE

TAMAR. Hey, there, Henry! This is a surprise.

HENRY. I hate how in New York people don't just drop by so I thought, what the hell, I'd just drop by, no phone call, no text, no nothing. And so I did. Here I am. And I brought breakfast. Bagels and lox. And there's something I want to talk to you about…

JIM. *(Offstage.)* Hey, Tamar! Do you have a towel?

HENRY. What? Who's that?

TAMAR. My ex. Jim.

HENRY. You mean the married guy?

TAMAR. No, the guy before that. He needed a couch to crash on. Don't worry about Jim. You're the only peegdog who gets to share my bed these days.

(She kisses him, takes the bagel, and exits.)

HENRY.

TRUE, SHE'S A NEUROTIC
TRUE, SHE'S IN THERAPY
TRUE, I MIGHT BE PSYCHOTIC
TO WANT TO PROPOSE SO FAST
LOVE IS A RISK
BUT THIS FEELS SO RIGHT
I MIGHT SLIP A DISC
IF I WAIT ONE MORE NIGHT

(Lights shift. He walks the streets of New York.)

BUT HOW DO YOU KNOW THE RIGHT TIME TO PROPOSE?
DO YOU PRESS HER OR LEAVE IT TO FATE?

YOU THINK THAT SHE WANTS YOU TO ASK HER
SHE'S WAITING TO SET THE DATE
DO YOU FLY TO BEIJING
TO WHIP OUT THE RING?
DO YOU...WAIT!

Got it! The seen-it-before-but-still-it's-so-good-it-never-fails proposal! The iconic spot! The Empire State Building at midnight!

AT NIGHT WHILE THE BIG APPLE GLOWS
THAT'S THE RIGHT TIME TO PROPOSE

> *(He is atop the Empire State Building. He is thrown a bouquet of flowers from offstage. He paces nervously.)*

You're good-looking, you're smart, women love you. You're good-looking, you're smart, women love you. You're good-looking...

TAMAR. Henry?

HENRY. Oh, Tamar! Yes! Tamar!

TAMAR. I'm sorry I'm late. You'll never guess who I ran into?

HENRY. *(Overlapping.)* Listen, Tamar. I know we haven't known each other for a long time but –

TAMAR. *(Cutting him off.)* Henry. I'm trying to tell you something serious here. I just ran into Robert and it really freaked me out.

HENRY. Robert?

TAMAR. Yeah. The married guy.

HENRY. You mean you're twenty minutes late because you were hanging out with your ex-married boyfriend?

TAMAR. What? Don't you trust me?

HENRY. You know? I guess I don't.

TAMAR. Wow. Sheila screwed you up even more than I thought.

HENRY. No, this isn't about her. This is about you. And Cindy. And the married guy. And the guy in the towel!

TAMAR. I guess I should've expected this. See you around, Henry.

HENRY. Oh, no! Not so fast. You don't get to run away from this.

TAMAR. From what?

HENRY. From your feelings for me.

TAMAR. Excuse me?

HENRY. If you have any. I'm into this, OK? Out on a major emotional limb, about two short seconds from falling off a gi-normous cliff. Come on, Tamar. What's going on?

[MUSIC NO. 09 "LOW EXPECTATIONS"]

TAMAR.
> WHAT'S GOING ON?
> YOU REALLY WANT TO KNOW?

HENRY. Yeah. Tell me.

TAMAR.
> YOU REALLY WANT TO SEE THE SIDE
> I TRY MY DAMNDEST NOT TO SHOW?

HENRY. Please.

TAMAR.
> I FALL IN LOVE
> AND GIVE MY HEART –
> MY CUSTOMARY M.O.
> BUT TIME AFTER TIME
> IT FALLS APART
> SO I KEEP MY EXPECTATIONS LOW
>
> AND THERE ARE GUYS
> I DATE FOR FUN –
> I TRY TO GO WITH THE FLOW
> WE HAVE OUR LAUGHS
> BUT THEN THEY HIT AND RUN
> SO I KEEP MY EXPECTATIONS LOW
>
> WHEN I FEEL DEFEATED
> I GET OUT OF THE GAME
> AND SPEND SATURDAY NIGHTS ON MY OWN
> SOON I'M FEELING STRONGER
> AND NO LONGER ALONE

WHEN I'VE DRIED ALL MY TEARS
A NEW GUY APPEARS

HE PROMISES
A PERFECT LIFE –
A RING COMPLETES THE TABLEAU
BUT A HOTEL WILL DO
WHILE HE HIDES FROM HIS WIFE
AT TWO A.M. IT'S MOSTLY TOUCH AND GO
SO I KEEP MY EXPECTATIONS LOW

HENRY.

BUT YOU DESERVE SO MUCH MORE

TAMAR.

YOU'RE NOT LIKE THOSE GUYS

HENRY.

SOMEONE ALWAYS THERE

TAMAR.

YOU'RE NOT PLAYING HARD TO GET

HENRY.

SOMEONE WHO WILL ALWAYS CARE

TAMAR.

BUT IS MY HEART BEYOND REPAIR?

HENRY.

DON'T QUIT NOW

TAMAR.

CAN YOU FORGIVE EACH PAST MISTAKE?

HENRY.

I'VE MADE A FEW

TAMAR.

CAN WE AGREE TO TAKE THINGS SLOW?

HENRY.

SLOW IS GOOD, JUST SO YOU KNOW

TAMAR.

IF I GET TOO CLOSE
AND THE FLOODGATES BREAK
I'M SCARED I WON'T SURVIVE THE UNDERTOW

(**HENRY** *takes her hand.*)

HENRY.

BUT ISN'T THAT HOW WE GROW?

LET'S START AGAIN FROM HELLO

TAMAR.

WITH SOMEONE I TRUST

TAMAR & HENRY.

AND SO

MAYBE IT'S TIME TO LET GO

OF LOW

EXPECTATIONS

[MUSIC NO. 09A "SEGUE OUT OF LOW EXPECTATIONS"]

Scene Nine

HENRY. So there it is, no more proposals, just a good week of nice get to know each other time. Real communication. Dare I say it: Maturity. As Tamar and I get closer and closer to the reading, I can tell that Gwen's separation from Diana is really eating at her. It just hurts to see my best friend on such a downward spiral.

(He exits as the lights shift to **GWEN** *entering the apartment.)*

GWEN. You're good-looking, you're smart, women love you… You're good-looking, you're smart, women… Oh, man! What am I doing? She's still your wife! Just call!

(She punches in the number.)

Hey, Diana. It's me. Gwen. I guess I'll just leave *another* message. I was wondering if you were ready to meet up? I mean, we talked about taking off those six months and what do you know? It's been six months!

(French accent.) Ze time she does fly, huh?

Anyway, I was wondering how you felt about it, because I am doing really well. Thriving, actually. The play was a big hit. Totally massive. If you can believe it, a producer's interested. I'd sure like to talk to you about it. I don't know if you've gotten all of these messages, but I'm sorry. Really sorry. Really, REALLY, SORRY! Jesus Christ, how many times do I have to say it? Do I have to tattoo it on my fucking forehead? Because I'm trying here! Remember what Dr. Fensterheim said? About building bridges over the river of our mutual respect? OK, what I did was wrong. But some would argue that it was *your* utter disregard of my creative endeavors that drove me to do it. I know we're not supposed to attach blame, but it's YOUR *FAULT*, OK? And like I've said, I've been THRIVING! Do you have any idea how many women I've hooked up with in the past months? My phone won't stop ringing!

(The landline rings.)

GWEN. Ah, speak of the devil. The landline!

[MUSIC NO. 09B "OBSCENE PHONE CALL #3"]

WOMAN'S VOICE.

I WANNA DO YOU ON THE DINING ROOM TABLE!

GWEN. *(Into landline.)* Ah, Henry told me you've been calling.

(Into cell phone.) Did you hear that, Diana? THRIVING!

> *(She speaks to the dining room table lady but neglects to hang up her cell.)*

So why don't you tell me a little bit about yourself?

WOMAN'S VOICE.

I WANNA DO YOU ON THE –

GWEN. Oh, god! Stop! Just stop! I thought I could do this but I just can't! I don't want sex on some random slab of wood! I'm barely holding it together here! I'm a bridge builder! I'm lost without my wife! Don't you get that? My wife!

> *(The person on the other end has hung up.)*

Hello? Hello?

> *(**HENRY** enters, shocked to see **GWEN** so low. She is still holding her cell phone. She is in tears.)*

HENRY. She'll come back.

[MUSIC NO. 09C "HENRY COMFORTS GWEN"]

GWEN. You really think so?

HENRY. Yeah. I know it.

> *(He hugs her as the lights go to black.)*

Scene Ten

(A mini stage is wheeled on with a poster reading "The Green Light." We are at HENRY's reading.)

HENRY. Hey, everyone. I'm Henry Mann, the author of this here little reading. Just a few words before we begin. First, this musical of mine, *The Green Light*, is based on a book you may have heard of: *The Great Gatsby*. In the interest of giving it a modern context, I took some liberties. So I'm hoping that you'll just go with me and I'm also hoping that nobody from the Fitzgerald estate is here. Anyway, I'd like to say a big thanks to my cast and my music director. But I really couldn't have pulled this off without my co-producer who did so much of the legwork.

(He peers into the audience.)

Is Tamar out there? Uh, Tamar? OK, so Tamar's running late, but you can say hi after the show. We'll have some refreshments and a brief talkback. I think that's it, except to thank my bestie Gwen for filling in at the last second for the actor who had to take...a personal day.

(A beat.)

OK, so there weren't any cell phones during the Roaring Twenties, so please silence yours. Thanks.

(He reaches into his pocket, unfolds a piece of paper, and reads.)

And now, without further ado, here is the show that dares to rethink a timeless classic! The show that brings Cuban elan to West Egg gentility!
(Rolls the "r.") The Green Light!

[MUSIC NO. 10 "THE GREEN LIGHT"]

(JAY GATSBY enters with a flourish. He is played by GWEN holding a script. GATSBY is dressed in a wild pink suit and sings with a Cuban accent.)

GATSBY.

MY PINK SUIT! PINK SUIT!
THERE'S NO SUBSTITUTE FOR MY PINK SUIT!

(**DAISY BUCHANAN** *enters.*)

My beautiful Daisy Buchanan! Let me show you around my home.

DAISY. *Oh, Jay!*

GATSBY. (*Hispanic accent.*) No, Chay.

DAISY. Of course, *Chay.*

GATSBY. Now come. I make a party, just for you.

MAMBO!

(**GATSBY** *and* **DAISY** *dance wildly. The music becomes more Latin, then it morphs into something twelve-tone and humorously experimental.*)

DAISY. Oh, Chay! Take me to your orgiastic future!

GATSBY & DAISY.

MAMBO!

HENRY. (*Stands and faces the audience.*) As you can see, the show wasn't exactly *West Side Story.* Worse, as the actors did their thing, Tamar never showed. Then I got a text.

(*A beat.*)

She was going back to Robert, the married guy.

DAISY. Careful, Chay! Watch for the ashen, fantastic figure gliding through the amorphous trees!

(*There is a gunshot.* **HENRY** *and* **GATSBY** *clutch their chests as* **GATSBY** *disappears upstage.*)

HENRY.

SO WE BEAT ON, BOATS AGAINST THE CURRENT
BORNE BACK CEASELESSLY INTO THE PAST!
THE PAST! THE PAST!

(*He falls onto his couch as the scene shifts to his apartment.*)

Scene Eleven

(Lights up on **MRS. MANN** *standing over* **HENRY**, *who is slumped on his couch.)*

MRS. MANN. I told you, you should've stuck with the teacher.

HENRY. Thanks, Mom. Real helpful right now.

MRS. MANN. Now I left the chicken in the kitchen. And I changed your sheets.

HENRY. Thanks, Mom. Thanks for stopping by.

(**MRS. MANN** *gives* **HENRY** *several kisses on the cheek.)*

MRS. MANN. Do you know what you need, Henry? Someone caring.

HENRY. Duly noted.

MRS. MANN. Someone to make sure you get your shirts pressed.

HENRY. Got it.

MRS. MANN. That your food is warm!

HENRY. Yes.

MRS. MANN. That your bed is made. It's what every man wants deep down, isn't it? The kind of unconditional love only a mother can provide. And I do happen to be available.

HENRY. Get out!

MRS. MANN. Take a joke, Henry. I just want you to find a girl who cares about you as much as I do.

HENRY. Thanks, Mom. But I think that might be impossible.

MRS. MANN. *(With a smile.)* Call the teacher.

(She exits. **HENRY** *hesitates, then picks up the phone. He dials. Hears a message.)*

CHRISTINE. *(Pre-recorded.)* Yeah, hi, it's me, Christine. Christine Warriner? OK, so I'm out now. You know what to do!

(**HENRY** *is about to speak, then hangs up.* **GWEN** *enters.)*

GWEN. Who you calling?

HENRY. Doesn't matter. You'll never believe what just happened.

GWEN. What?

HENRY. My mother! She just suggested that I marry her. Or someone like her anyway.

GWEN. You could do worse.

HENRY. Don't you see, Gwen? Sheila's wedding is next week! I don't have anyone to take!

GWEN. You can always take yoga girl.

[MUSIC NO. 10A "YOGA GIRL CHORDS"]

(**HENRY** and **GWEN** *watch yoga girl.*)

HENRY. No.

GWEN. Or bring your niece.

HENRY. Jill? She's eight!

GWEN. Hey, listen, I know you're still torn up over Tamar. But good riddance, OK? A beret? A Cuban Jay Gatsby? You had some good stuff in that show but her ideas turned it into a circus. You have talent. Revise your novel. Write more kids' poems. Start another show. Stick with it.

HENRY. Thanks.

GWEN. OK, this is how it's going to work. You've been hiding out here eating chips for a week. Another few days and you'll be a documentary. First, you will bathe. Then you will shave and put on the clean clothes I laid out on your bed. Then we are going out to celebrate.

HENRY. Why?

GWEN. It's your birthday, idiot. Get dressed!

Scene Twelve

[MUSIC NO. 10B "THE SLEEPY WHEEL"]

(Lights up on a dive folk bar.)

WEIRD STONED VOICE-OVER. Ladies and gentlemen, welcome to the Sleepy Wheel, Avenue D's hottest folk bar. Our show will begin in five minutes.

(HENRY and GWEN enter.)

HENRY. Christ! This place is farther east than Cambodia. What are we doing here?

GWEN. Just have a seat and all will be revealed.

HENRY. All will be revealed? You've been acting weird since we left the apartment.

GWEN. Well, I have been meaning to tell you something. And I wanted to make sure you had changed your underwear before I did. You know how I've been calling Diana.

HENRY. Yeah?

GWEN. Well...she finally took me back.

HENRY. What? That's great.

GWEN. She accidentally overheard my breakdown the other day. I guess she finally realized how much I missed her.

HENRY. So Diana forgave you?

GWEN. Yeah, but I know it isn't going to be easy. I have work to do.

HENRY. Yeah, you do.

[MUSIC NO. 10C "OBSCENE PHONE CALL #4"]

WOMAN'S VOICE.
I WANNA DO YOU ON THE DINING ROOM TABLE!

HENRY. Wait! What's going on? Is that weird lady calling your cell now?

GWEN. Nope. I use it now as my ringtone.
(Into the phone.) Yeah, hey, Diana. Your place? Milk? You got it. I'll see you in a couple of hours. Bye.

WEIRD STONED VOICE-OVER. OK, welcome once again to the Sleepy Wheel. Now introducing our hottest new attraction. Christine Warriner!

> (**CHRISTINE** *enters, holding a guitar, and takes a seat on a stool on a stage.*)

HENRY. Oh, my god!
(To **GWEN**.*)* Jerk.

CHRISTINE. Thanks...thanks for coming out tonight. This is my first time playing live in a place like this so...well, I just wanted to say that. OK, like the guy said I'm Christine. Christine Warriner. OK, so I'm going to start with an original tune. Here goes.

[MUSIC NO. 10D "IT'S ONLY A FIRST DATE – REPRISE"]

(Sings a folk version.)

MAYBE YOU WILL NEVER KNOW HIS FAV'RITE BAND AT WOODSTOCK
HIS FAV'RITE FILM BY HITCHCOCK
THE BOOKS HE'S READ, HIS TOUCH IN BED...

HENRY. Oh, damn, damn, damn...

GWEN. What?

HENRY. I need air! *(He gets up.)*

GWEN. Get your butt back in the chair!

CHRISTINE.

FOR IT'S ONLY A DANCE
IT'S ONLY A MEAL
IT'S ONLY A GUY
SO COME ON, GET REAL
THERE'S NO CHANCE IN HELL
THAT HE FEELS WHAT YOU FEEL...

'CAUSE IT'S ONLY A FIRST DATE
NOTHING MORE

> (*Recorded applause fills the theater, joined by* **HENRY** *and* **GWEN**.*)

Thank you.

GWEN. *(Indicating that* **HENRY** *should talk to her.)* Come on!

HENRY. Oh, no! That song was about us. Our date.

GWEN. That just means she likes you, man. Go talk to her.

HENRY. But I got slow-dance wood, Gwen! Slow-dance wood!

GWEN. That's got to be a rite of passage. Forget it.

HENRY. I never even called her.

GWEN. So you messed up. Apologize.

HENRY. She said she was dating someone.

GWEN. Boy, are you late to the party. That petered out.

HENRY. You think I still have a chance?

GWEN. Sure I do. I bet you could probably even bring her to Sheila's wedding.

HENRY. Oh, forget Sheila.

GWEN. Forget Sheila?

HENRY. Yeah, I've been thinking. I don't need to prove anything to her, right? I'll go to the wedding alone. Wish her well and that'll be it.

> (**SHEILA** *appears in a wedding veil, blows* **HENRY** *a goodbye kiss, and exits.)*

GWEN. Good for you. Like I said, Christine is the one you should be with anyway.

HENRY. We did get along really well. I mean, it was easy.

GWEN. That's great, Henry. But take it from someone who's been through the pits of hell, relationships aren't always easy.

HENRY. I know that.

GWEN. Do you?

[MUSIC NO. 11 "THE UNROMANTIC THINGS"]

Have you ever really listened to the vows at all those weddings you went to?

THERE'S STUFF ABOUT LOVE

SOME WORDS ABOUT CARING
SOME LINES ABOUT SHARING
WHILE THE BRIDE DABS HER EYES

'CAUSE THEN YOU GO HOME
WRITE SOME THANK YOU NOTES
FIGHT OVER YOUR REMOTES
AND LEARN TO COMPROMISE

IT'S NOT ALWAYS PRETTY OR ROMANTIC
YOU NEVER KNOW WHAT STUFF TOMORROW BRINGS
SO YOU FIND WHAT'S PRETTY AND ROMANTIC
IN THE UNROMANTIC THINGS

YOU EAT A LATE MEAL
YOU FIN'LLY WATCH *MAD MEN*
YOU GOTTA BE GLAD WHEN
YOU CAN GET HER IN THE MOOD

YOU WISH FOR MORE TIME
TIME TO LIVE, TO BE WILD
THEN YOU HAVE A CHILD...
AND YOU'RE REALLY SCREWED

IT'S NOT ALWAYS PRETTY OR ROMANTIC
NO MORE DATES, NO MORE FLINGS
SO YOU FIND WHAT'S PRETTY AND ROMANTIC

HENRY.

IN THE MEALS, THE CHORES

GWEN.

IN THE FLOSSING, IN THE SNORES
IN THE UNROMANTIC THINGS

HENRY. God, Gwen! You make it sound so frigging depressing.

GWEN. Yeah, it is. But it's also sort of great. And I miss it.

THE STUFF ABOUT LOVE
THE STUFF ABOUT CARING
THE STUFF ABOUT SHARING
IT TURNS OUT IT'S TRUE

MORE OFTEN THAN NOT
YOU'LL ONLY READ IN BED

THE THINGS LEFT UNSAID
BRING HER CLOSE TO YOU

IT'S NOT ALWAYS SEXY OR EXCITING

HENRY.

BUT THERE'S PLENTY IN STORE TO RECOMMEND

GWEN.

WHAT'S MORE THRILLING OR INVITING
THAN SPENDING YOUR LIFE

HENRY.

WITH A WONDERFUL WIFE

GWEN & HENRY.

AND A BUCKET OF WINGS?
ALL THOSE UNROMANTIC THINGS

HENRY. I can do that. I like wings! And I love you. But you know what, Gwen?

GWEN. Yeah. It's time. I need to move out. I need to be with Diana.

HENRY. Yeah, you do. Hey...thanks for taking care of me.

GWEN. Anytime. Now *you* need to get your butt over to Christine. And don't propose in the next ten minutes. Baby steps are fine. But make something happen.

> (**HENRY** *hugs* **GWEN,** *then heads toward* **CHRISTINE.**)

WHAT'S MORE PRETTY OR ROMANTIC
THAN TO START ANEW
WITH A DINING ROOM TABLE FOR TWO
HAPPILY TIED TO APRON STRINGS?
ALL THOSE UNROMANTIC THINGS

> (**GWEN** *calls Diana.*)

Hey baby, I'm on my way.

> (**HENRY** *approaches* **CHRISTINE.**)

HENRY. Hey. Great set.

CHRISTINE. *(Distant.)* Oh, Henry. Thanks.

HENRY. You said you wrote folk songs and you do. And they're great.

CHRISTINE. Thanks.

HENRY. OK, you know, this might sound silly after all this time, but remember how we said we'd play some hoops in the park one afternoon? I was wondering if you'd like to do it. I mean, play hoops. With me.

CHRISTINE. Henry...

HENRY. I know I screwed up and I'm so sorry. About everything. Couldn't we just X out all the bad stuff and start over?

(He looks her in the eyes.)

Christine?

CHRISTINE. What are you staring at?

HENRY. What? Nothing.

CHRISTINE. Yes, you are. You're staring at something. Just like you did on our date.

HENRY. No, no.

(He dabs a lash off of her cheek.)

It's just you have an eyelash on your cheek.

(He silently makes a wish and softly blows away the eyelash.)

CHRISTINE. Oh...

HENRY. So two o'clock, tomorrow. You know the courts at Riverside? I'll be there.

CHRISTINE. Henry...don't get your hopes up.

(She exits.)

Scene Thirteen

[MUSIC NO. 12 "KEEPING MY EYE ON THE BALL"]

HENRY. Yeah, great. I guess I shouldn't be surprised, given the last few months. You might say I've made some pretty debatable decisions. I fell for the wrong girl while pining for my ex-girl and to top it off, I treated the right girl like crap. But maybe...maybe...there's still hope?

KEEPING MY EYE ON THE BALL
KEEPING MY EYE ON THE BALL THIS TIME
DRIBBLE TWICE
TAKE AN EASY SHOT
MAKE A HIGH-PERCENTAGE PASS

KEEPING MY EYE ON THE BALL
MAYBE I WON'T TAKE A FALL THIS TIME
PLAY IT NICE
CHOOSE MY SPOT
BEFORE STEPPING ON THE GAS

NO MORE JUMPING TO CONCLUSIONS
NO MORE ANTICIPATING FATE
NO MORE IMAGINING MY DAUGHTER'S SMILE
OR MY BRIDE-TO-BE WALKING DOWN THE AISLE
BEFORE I'VE EVEN HAD A SECOND DATE!

KEEPING MY EYE ON THE BALL
KEEPING MY EYE ON THE BALL THIS TIME
WATCH THE CLOCK, GIVE THE BALL A SPIN
TAKE IT STEP BY STEP
FORGET THE PAST
MAKE A MOVE
BUT NOT TOO FAST
HE SHOOTS, HE SCORES!
IT'S MY TURN TO WIN

What did Gwen say?

GWEN. *(From the wings.)* Baby steps, Henry!

GWEN & HENRY. Baby steps!

HENRY.

> FIRST STEP: I PACE, I GROAN
> SECOND STEP: REACH FOR THE PHONE
> THIRD STEP: HYPERVENTILATE
> FOURTH STEP: I TAKE THE BAIT

(Into his cell phone.) Hello...? Christine...? I'm here. By the baskets! Where I've been every Saturday for the past month! Guess what? I have a meeting with a kids' editor about my poems. Anyway, you've gotten my messages, right? Just so you know, I'm going to be here every Saturday until you show up and kick my ass!

> FIFTH STEP: I'M ALREADY SCREWED
> ANOTHER FRIGGIN' MESSAGE AND MY MIND'S UNGLUED:
> LIVING OUT OUR WEDDING DAY
> WHO WILL GIVE THE BRIDE AWAY
> THINKING WHAT TO NAME OUR KIDS
> IMAGINING MY MOVIE BIDS
> NO!
> BABY STEPS
> TAKE IT SLOW
>
> NO MORE CATALOGUING VIRTUES
> NO MORE MATURITY DEFERRED
> LOVE IS CHERISHING A PERSON'S QUIRKS
> THAT'S PART OF WHY A MARRIAGE WORKS
> THE HEART MUST LEARN TO HAVE THE FINAL WORD
>
> KEEPING MY EYE ON THE BALL
> KEEPING MY EYE ON THE BALL THIS TIME
> SET ASIDE THOSE WEDDING RINGS
> EMBRACE THE UNROMANTIC THINGS
> DON'T WORRY WHAT THE FUTURE BRINGS...

> *(A new woman enters, **NATALIE**, **HENRY**'s age. She holds a yoga bag.)*

NATALIE. Hey, do you ever play with other people?

HENRY. Huh?

NATALIE. You're here every weekend, right? I've seen you shooting around but never in a game.

HENRY. Oh, yeah, I've been waiting for someone.

>   *(A beat.)*

But not anymore, I guess... I'm Henry.

NATALIE. Natalie. Nice to meet you.

HENRY. You, too. So... What's that?

(Realizing who she might be.) A yoga bag?!

NATALIE. Hey, don't you live across the way? With your girlfriend?

HENRY. No, no, just a friend. And she moved out.

NATALIE. Oh.

HENRY. You really noticed me?

NATALIE. The apartments are pretty close.

HENRY. So you wanna play? A little one-on-one?

>   *(He flips her the ball.)*

NATALIE. Oh, I'm not very good.

HENRY. Me neither. We'll just take things...slow.

NATALIE. I can live with that, Henry. Catch.

>   *(She throws him the ball. The strains of "Keeping My Eye On The Ball" rise and...)*
>
>   *(Curtain.)*

[MUSIC NO. 13 "BOWS/EXIT"]

The End

www.ingramcontent.com/pod-product-compliance
Lightning Source LLC
Chambersburg PA
CBHW070358120726
47909CB00008B/2897